# ONE
# SMART
# GOOSE

For David

LIBRARY OF CONGRESS CATALOGING-IN-PUBLICATION DATA
Church, Caroline. One smart goose / Caroline Jayne Church. p. cm.
Summary: A goose who likes to wash in a muddy pond is teased by the other geese, until they realize that he is the only one not chased by the fox.
[1. Geese—Fiction. 2. Foxes—Fiction. 3. Cleanliness—Fiction. 4. Intellect—Fiction.] I. Title. PZ7.C4650n 2005 [E]—dc22 2004006847
ISBN 0-439-68765-9
10 9 8 7 6 5 4 3 2 1     09 08 07 06 05

Printed in China
Reinforced Binding for Library Use
First Orchard Books edition, April 2005

# ONE SMART GOOSE

Caroline Jayne Church

ORCHARD BOOKS / NEW YORK
AN IMPRINT OF SCHOLASTIC INC.

Down on the farm lived a gaggle of geese.
They were shiny and clean.
Even their beaks gleamed.

One little goose splashed alone in a muddy pond.
He wasn't shiny or clean.
And his beak certainly did not gleam.

The other geese laughed at him.
"Look at that dirty goose!" they honked.

Most of the time all the geese led a
very happy life. But when the full moon
shone they would tremble with fear.

A full moon meant
only one thing . . .

. . . the fox would come!
And **whoosh!**
Down the hill he'd
chase all the geese,
through the woods,
and all around
the farm.

The fox chased all the geese that is, except one.
He never chased the lonely, little goose.

One morning after a very bad chase, the geese had just had enough. It was time for a talk.

"Why doesn't the fox ever chase you?" they demanded.
"Have you got a secret you're not telling us?"

"No," said the dirty, little goose. "It's because of my muddy feathers. They blend into the shadows so the fox can't see me. Not even by the light of a full moon."

All the geese looked at each other . . .

. . . and ran to the nearest muddy pond!

Time went by and all the happy,
muddy geese pecked away
on the hillside.

All that is, except one.

The lonely, little goose watched the sky.
It was heavy and gray. He shivered.
It could mean only one thing.

He called to the others and tried
to explain, but they wouldn't listen.

So he set off alone once more,
this time to find a clean, clear pond.

There, he washed and scrubbed,

scrubbed
and washed,

until all his feathers
were clean and gleaming.

That night the moon rose,
full and round. And **whoosh!**
The fox chased all the geese once again.

All the geese that is, except one.
The fox didn't see the lonely, little goose.

And he didn't see his
foot either. **Bam!**
with a **bump** and a **thump**
he fell into the snow and rolled down the hill.
The fox rolled faster and faster . . .

. . . further and further,
    far, far away, out of sight.
        "He's gone!" cried the geese.
            "I don't think he'll be back either,"
                smiled the smart little goose.

"Oh, thank you!" said the geese. And for the first time, the little goose felt like part of the gaggle, and was never lonely again.